The  Show

by Rachel Johns
illustrated by Meredith Thomas

Harcourt
SCHOOL PUBLISHERS

Printed in Mexico

ISBN 10: 0-15-350642-3
ISBN 13: 978-0-15-350642-0

Ordering Options
ISBN 10: 0-15-350599-0 (Grade 2 On-Level Collection)
ISBN 13: 978-0-15-350599-7 (Grade 2 On-Level Collection)
ISBN 10: 0-15-357823-8 (package of 5)
ISBN 13: 978-0-15-357823-6 (package of 5)

1 2 3 4 5 6 7 8 9 10   050   15 14 13 12 11 10 09 08 07 06

Farmer was getting Goat ready
for the country show. Farmer brought
him a thick blanket. He brushed
Goat's coat until it was shiny. He fed
him spinach.

"I would like a thick blanket,"
grumbled Chicken.

"I would like some spinach,"
moaned Cow.

"I would like my coat brushed,"
groaned Horse.

4

"I have had enough of your complaining!" said Cat, early one morning. "It's impossible to get any sleep around here."

The animals looked at Cat in surprise.

"Instead of moaning," said Cat, "why don't you do something about it?"

"What *can* we do?" asked the animals.

Cat sighed. "Talk to Farmer," he continued, "and make him understand why you are unhappy."

That afternoon, the animals went to the farmhouse. They knocked on Farmer's door. He could not believe the animals all wanted to be looked after like Goat.

"That's impossible," he said. "I don't have the time."

The animals went back to the
barnyard feeling quite sorry for
themselves. Cat listened to them
complain again.

"Why don't you go on strike?"
he suggested. "Don't do anything for
Farmer until he does what you want."

The next day, Farmer went to
get the milk from Cow.

"No milk?" Farmer exclaimed.

"I have no time to make milk,"
said Cow.

Then, Farmer went to ride Horse to the market, but Horse wouldn't move.

"No ride today?" he exclaimed.

"I have no time to take you there," said Horse.

Finally, Farmer went to get eggs from Chicken's nest.

"No eggs?" he exclaimed.

"I have no time to lay eggs," said Chicken.

Farmer realized how much he needed the animals. Without their help, there would be no eggs to eat and no milk to drink. He would not be able to go to the market.

The next morning, Farmer brought spinach for all the animals. They had thick blankets. He brushed their coats until they were shiny.

Cow gave milk, and Chicken laid eggs. Horse took Farmer to the market.

That afternoon, Farmer took all the animals to the country show.

"What wonderful animals you have," the judge said. He gave them each a blue ribbon.

That night, Cat had the best sleep ever.

Think Critically

1. How do you think this story would be different without Cat?

2. Why did Farmer change during the story?

3. Which character in the story would you like to be? Why?

4. Why do you think Cat would have had the best sleep ever?

5. Do you think Cat was smart? Why or why not?

 Social Studies

Write a Paragraph In the story, Farmer gets milk from Cow. Write a paragraph about why milk is important.

 **School-Home Connection** Tell a family member about *The Country Show*. Talk about all the things that you might see at a country show.